BILLY AND THE MINI MONSTERS

Monsters Go Party!

ZANNA DAVIDSON

Illustrated by
MELANIE WILLIAMSON

Reading consultant: Alison Kelly

Meet Billy...

Billy was just
an ordinary boy
living an ordinary
life, until
ONE NIGHT
he found
five
**MINI
MONSTERS**
in his sock drawer.

Gloop   Peep   Fang-Face   Captain Snott   Trumpet

Then he saved their lives, and they swore never to leave him.

We give you the Secret-Hairy-Snot-Tooth Oath of Devotion.

We're awesome!

And fun!

And SCARY!

Are we scary? I'm not sure I'm very scary.

One thing was certain – Billy's life would never be the same **AGAIN**...

Contents

Chapter 1
Party Time

Party!

Billy was
very excited.
It was his friend
Jack's birthday,
and he was going to
his dressing-up party.

Unfortunately, his little sister Ruby was friends with Jack's little sister, so she was coming too.

But Billy found it very HARD to
be nice to Ruby.

She destroyed
his toys...

...ruined his games...

...and always wanted to
play in his bedroom.

There was **NO WAY** Billy was
going to let Ruby into his bedroom.

Ruby had to learn that Billy's bedroom was PRIVATE.

Because Billy had his
TOP SECRET
pets to protect.

The MINI MONSTERS!

"We can't wait to come to the party!" said Captain Snott. "I've been practising the birthday song."

Happy Snottday to you, Happy Snottday to youuuuu...

Er, that's not how it goes.

The Mini Monsters had been busy dreaming about Jack's birthday party **ALL WEEK**.

"I'm sorry but you can't come to the party," said Billy. "Not after what's happened the last few times."

The Mini Monsters were always getting into trouble:

At the swimming pool...

Fang-Face and Captain Snott nearly drowning.

Gloop being SUCKED down the drain.

At home...

All of the monsters getting trapped in the washing machine.

At school...

Peep ending up in a hamster cage...

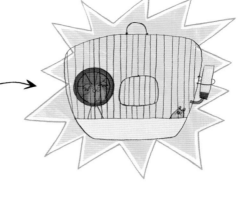

...and Trumpet sinking in a vat of baked beans.

And at the airport...

Gloop and Trumpet getting lost with the luggage.

Billy had caused so much trouble trying to rescue them he'd had **NO**

TV

FOR A

WEEK.

Billy knew if the Mini Monsters came to the party, he would end up in **EVEN MORE** trouble.

"I'll make it up to you," said Billy. "I'll bring you back some cake!"

I want you to stay RIGHT here.

We promise.

"Bye," called Billy. And he went out of his room, and shut the door.

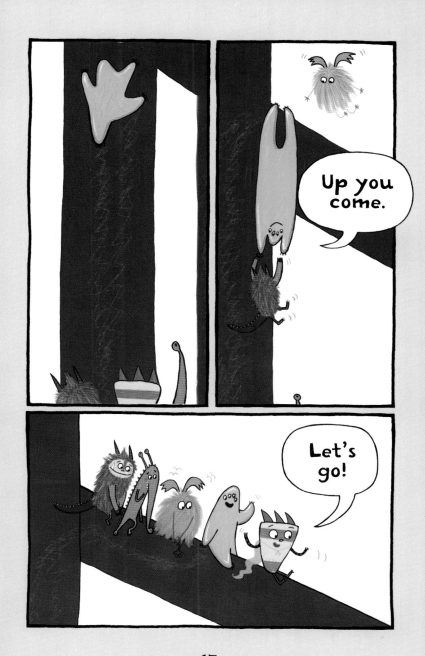

18

19

Chapter 2
The Magic Show

Billy sat down with his friends.
There was going to be a magic show.

"Let the show **begin**!"
said the magician.

He magicked
FLAMES
from his
wand…

…made amazing
balloon animals…

…and even sawed the birthday boy in half.

Don't worry - I'll put him back together.

"And now for my final and favourite trick – the rabbit in the hat!" the magician said.

The magician tapped his hat three times...

one

two

three

Then he put his hand **inside**...

and pulled out...

29

Chapter 3
Up and Away

Billy *rushed* over to the magician. He had to get Fang-Face back. But Jack's mum was making everyone go outside.

Time for the treasure hunt in the garden.

There was nothing Billy could do. But then, outside, he saw...

He had to rescue them.
What if they were…

…eaten by a bird…

…or **swept**
out to sea…

…or carried into

OUTER
SPACE?

Billy tried catching the balloon,
but he couldn't jump high enough.

He tried spearing the balloon with a stick…

He **missed**.

"This isn't good," thought Billy. Then the wind started to blow harder. He ran this way…

…and that way, chasing the balloon across the garden. But the balloon kept slipping from his grasp.

The balloon was heading over the garden wall... but, at the last moment, its string caught in a tree. "Phew!" said Billy.

A very

tall

tree.

"Oh no!" said Billy as he looked up. There was only one thing for it.

He took a deep breath and began to climb.

By now, a small crowd had gathered beneath him.

"Go on, Billy!" cried Jack.

No one's ever made it to the top of that tree before.

Careful, Billy!

Billy kept on climbing. Even though the branches were getting very thin...

He reached across for the Mini Monsters.

That was fun!

Shall we do it again?

The branch creaked and swayed in the wind. Billy wondered if he was going to **FALL**. Slowly, carefully, he picked up the Mini Monsters.

By the time Billy got back down, his legs felt all w\ob\b\ly.

Ruby was watching him very closely. "What's in your hand?" she asked.

I can't tell you. It's a secret.

"Well, I've got a secret too," said Ruby. "It's small and hairy, but really amazing. I'll tell you mine if you tell me yours."

Normally, Billy wasn't interested in Ruby's secrets, but when she said **SMALL AND HAIRY**, he couldn't help wondering if Ruby HAD found a Mini Monster? Were they *all* at the party?

"Okay," he said at last. "Tell me yours first."

I've found a little pink hamster. **WITH WINGS.**

Where is it?

Not telling...

...until you tell me **YOUR** secret.

Ruby's secret sounded a lot like Peep. Billy *had* to get him back.

"This is a very important secret," said Billy. "Here goes."

41

Chapter 4
Peep the Doll

"Wow!" said Ruby, when Billy had finished telling her his secret.

Is that really true?

Shh!

"You've got little pet monsters that are **ALIVE!**

Can I meet them?"

Billy looked around to make sure no one was watching.

Then he **OPENED** his hand…

"*WOW!*"
said Ruby again,
and she bent
down to give
Captain Snott
a kiss.

He blushed.

Then she patted Trumpet
on the head.

"And there are *more* of them?"
Ruby asked excitedly.

Billy nodded. "I need your help finding them. This is what they look like…" He took out a pencil and some paper.

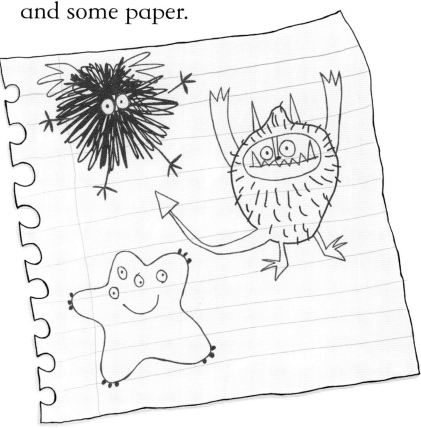

"Ooh!" said Ruby. "The hairy one's my hamster! Follow me!"

"Remember," said Billy, as they went into the house.

No one must realize what we're up to.

We're a team!

Together, they **CREPT UPSTAIRS...**

ALONG THE CORRIDOR...

And into Jack's sister's room.

"In there," whispered Ruby. "In the dolls' house."

"Quick!" Ruby
called through the door.
"Someone's coming."

50

Billy just had time to slip the
Mini Monsters into his cape pocket,
when Jack's mum came
into the room.

What are
you doing
in here?

"I was just showing Billy the
dolls' house," said Ruby. "Billy
loves dolls' houses."

Billy nodded.

Jack's mum looked **SUSPICIOUS**.

Billy looked at the tea table and groaned. "And I think it's about to get worse..."

A little while earlier...

Oooh! Yummy!

54

56

My friend!

57

Chapter 5
Jelly and Cake

"Oh no!" thought Billy.

He could see Gloop on the tea table **pretending to be a jelly**.

He was very good at it.

So good, that if he wasn't careful, someone was going to **EAT HIM**.

But before Billy could grab
Gloop, all the other kids
started coming in for tea.

Just then, Jack came forward.
He was headed for

THE JELLY.

Billy leaned over to pick up
Gloop… but Gloop wouldn't
let go of the jelly.

Jack reached for the plate…
so Billy picked up the whole jelly.

Billy was
trying to
move Gloop,
but nothing
was working.

"**Billy**," said Jack's mum
again. "I asked you to put that
jelly back."

Gloop!
That's not
another monster.
It's food.

I don't
believe you.

Jack's mum picked up a big spoon.

"Oh no!" thought Billy. "She's going to **CUT** Gloop in half!"

"I'll have it," said Ruby. She grabbed hold of Gloop and a large lump of jelly, and put them both on her plate.

Where are your manners?

"I'm going to have to tell your mother about this…"

Billy looked round and realized the parents were already starting to arrive. And there was his mum, coming into the dining room.

Luckily, just then, Jack's dad called, "Get ready for the cake."

Everyone stopped looking at the
jelly and started singing "Happy
Birthday", except for Captain Snott.

Billy could hear his little voice
piping up from inside his cape.

All the children leaned forward
to watch Jack blow out the candles.
Jack took a deep breath and...

65

Jack's mum **fainted**.
The parents screamed.

In all the confusion, Billy grabbed Fang-Face and Gloop stuffed them both inside his cape.

"That's all of them," Billy whispered to Ruby.

Party's over.

69

70

Chapter 6
A Monster Party

When Billy and Ruby got home, their mum **marched** them into the house.

"We're sorry, Mum," said Billy, "but the good news," he added, grinning, "is that Ruby and I are now BEST FRIENDS."

73

74

As soon as they got upstairs, Billy shut his bedroom door.

"Thanks for all your help today, Ruby," he said. "Maybe little sisters aren't so bad after all."

Ruby grinned.

Shut your eyes, Peep.

"There's something we've got to do…" Billy whispered.

Thirty minutes later, Billy opened
the sock drawer again, and...

SURPRISE!

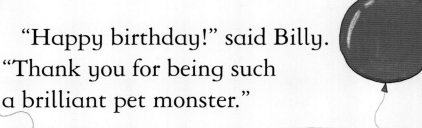

"Happy birthday!" said Billy. "Thank you for being such a brilliant pet monster."

I promise never to call you a hamster again.

"Then it really is my BEST birthday ever," said Peep.

All about the
MINI MONSTERS

FANG-FACE →

LIKES EATING:
socks, school ties,
paper, or anything
that comes his way.

SPECIAL SKILL:
has massive fangs.

SCARE FACTOR:
9/10

← GLOOP

LIKES EATING: cake.

SPECIAL SKILL:
very stre-e-e-e-tchy.
Gloop can also swallow
his own eyeballs and
make them reappear on
any part of his body.

SCARE FACTOR:
4/10

CAPTAIN SNOTT

LIKES EATING: bogeys.

SPECIAL SKILL:
can glow in the dark.

SCARE
FACTOR:
5/10

PEEP

LIKES EATING: very small flies.

SPECIAL SKILL: can fly (but
not very far, or very well).

SCARE FACTOR:
0/10 (unless you're afraid of
small hairy things)

TRUMPET →

LIKES EATING: cheese.

SPECIAL SKILL:
amazingly powerful
cheese-powered parps.

SCARE FACTOR:
7/10
(taking into
account his parps)

Designed by Brenda Cole
Edited by Becky Walker
Cover design by Hannah Cobley
Digital manipulation by John Russell

First published in 2017 by Usborne Publishing Ltd., Usborne House,
83-85 Saffron Hill, London EC1N 8RT, England. www.usborne.com
Copyright © 2017 Usborne Publishing Ltd. UKE

USBORNE YOUNG READING

BILLY AND THE MINI MONSTERS

Monsters in the Dark

by ZANNA DAVIDSON

Illustrated by MELANIE WILLIAMSON

USBORNE YOUNG READING

BILLY AND THE MINI MONSTERS

Monsters on the Loose

by ZANNA DAVIDSON

Illustrated by MELANIE WILLIAMSON

USBORNE YOUNG READING

BILLY AND THE MINI MONSTERS

Monsters to the Rescue

by ZANNA DAVIDSON

Illustrated by MELANIE WILLIAMSON

MONSTER fun for everyone!